And so it was that Mr Snow received a visit from Father Christmas.

"Hello, Mr Snow," said Father Christmas. "I have a job for you. A little boy in Australia called Ben has asked for a white Christmas. Do you think you can make his wish come true?"

"I think I know just the person who can," said Mr Snow, after a moment's thought.

"Excellent!" said Father Christmas. "You can borrow my sleigh. It's a rather long walk to Australia!"

Mr Snow packed his suitcase and set off for Australia.

On the way he picked up a very good friend of his, Little Miss Magic. It took them no time at all to get to Australia in Father Christmas's sleigh.

Ben was very excited when he saw Mr Snow and Little Miss Magic standing on his doorstep.

"Hello, Ben," said Little Miss Magic. "We're here to make your wish come true."

"I think we need to hurry up," said Mr Snow. "I'm starting to melt!"

So Little Miss Magic muttered some very magic words and suddenly the temperature dropped, huge grey clouds rolled over the horizon, and it began to snow.

Ben could not believe his eyes.

It snowed.

And it snowed.

And it snowed.

Everywhere was covered in a thick blanket of fluffy, white snow.

Ben ran inside his house and put on all his jumpers.

"Would you like to come for a ride in Father Christmas's flying sleigh?" asked Mr Snow.

"Yes please!" said Ben.

They climbed aboard and Mr Snow took off.

Ben looked in wonder at the snowy landscape below them.

But everywhere they went Ben began to notice the same thing.

The kangaroos, standing in the snowy outback, did not look very happy.

The crocodiles in the icy river did not look very happy.

And everyone on the snowy beach did not look very happy.

They looked very unhappy and very cold.

"Oh dear," sighed Ben. "I don't think anyone else wants the snow as much as I do. I think you'd better make it all go away."

So Little Miss Magic muttered some more very magic words and before you could say, "Hey Presto" the clouds had rolled away and the sun came out and melted all the snow.

Ben looked sadly at the puddles at his feet. And it was then that Mr Snow had an idea. "Why don't we fly to places where people do like snow?"

"Can we?" cried Ben.

"We certainly can," said Little Miss Magic.

And so they did just that.

They flew to Coldland and went sledging with
Mr Sneeze.

Then they visited Mr Bump and went ice skating.

"Do you know where they have more snow than anywhere else?" Mr Snow asked.

"Where?" asked Ben.

"At the North Pole!" said Mr Snow.

"That's where Father Christmas lives!" cried Ben.

"Indeed it is," said Mr Snow.

And that is how a little boy from Australia found himself at the North Pole in …

… a snowball fight with Mr Snow, Little Miss Christmas, Mr Christmas and Father Christmas!

And what a snowball fight it was!

"I'm sorry you didn't get to have a white Christmas in Australia," laughed Mr Snow, as his snowball hit Father Christmas's chest.

"But at least you did get to see one white Christmas …"

"... a white Father Christmas! We've turned him into a snowman!"